NORSE MYTHOLOGY FOR KIDS

Illustrated Myths of Gods, Goddesses, Giants, Dwarves, Elves, and other Fantastic Beings of the Viking Saga

By Monica Roy
Illustrations: Paloma Romero
Editor: Balázs Garda

Table of Contents

NORSE MYTHOLOGY.
WHAT IS IT ABOUT?

Long ago (about 750 BC), Northern Europe was populated by many tribes. They lived free and independent of each other, in villages made of huts. They used primitive tools and moved around on foot or in carts pulled by oxen or horses.

THE MYTHS

They also shared fantastic myths and tales. At that time, people didn't write them on paper, but told them verbally. This way, these myths passed on from one generation to the next about the time of the Vikings. They were finally written down during the Medieval age in two books called the Eddas.

ASGARD
ALFHEIM
MIDGARD
MUSPELL
VANAHEIM
NID
JOTUNHEIM
HELH
NIFLHEIM

YGGDRASIL
AND THE NINE WORLDS

One of the most fascinating myths is about how they imagine the universe was made.

They imagined the universe to have nine realms or "worlds". They were like nine different levels, leaning against a huge ash tree called Yggdrasil: the tree of the world.

At the top lived the gods, at the bottom was Hell, and in the middle, lived men.

The world where the gods live was called Ásaheimr. In this place, on the top of the

ASGARD

ALFHEIM

MIDGARD

mountains, the gods built their fortress, Asgard, with full of beautiful palaces and temples. This realm could only be reached by walking across a rainbow bridge.

At the bottom of the tree was a cold dark place, Hel, where the dead rested. It was under the rule of Hel, daughter of Loki, the god of chaos, evil, and lies.

Midgard was the world of men; it was in the center of the tree and can be compared to the planet Earth.

There was also a realm where the fire giants lived called Muspelheim, a region of constant fire.

The other worlds were:

Vanaheimr: the land of a family of gods called Vanir, where, among others, lived the gods of fertility, wisdom, and magical arts. The Vanir were a tribe of nature and fertility gods. For this reason, while the Aesir established their home in the high heavens, the Vanir preferred to live in contact with nature.

Jotunheimr: the realm of the giants Jötunn, and was located at the far ends of the world.

Álfheimr: the realm of the light elves (the Ljósálfar). It was located near Asgard.

Svartálfaheimr: the realm located underground. There dwelled the dark elves, Døkkálfar, and the dwarves, Dvergar.

Niflheimr: the world of mist and frost located

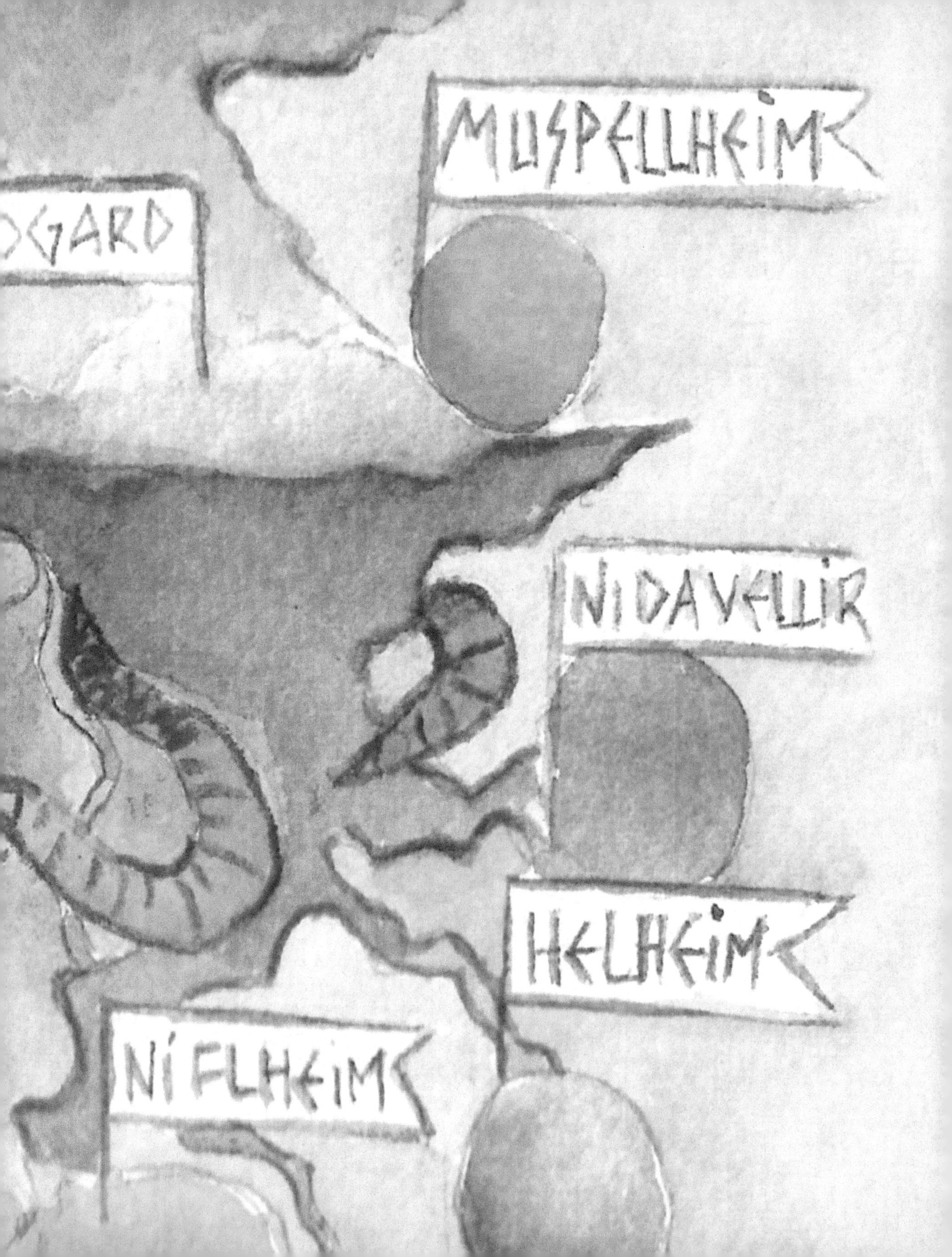

GARD
MUSPELLHEIM
NIDAVELLIR
HELHEIM
NIFLHEIM

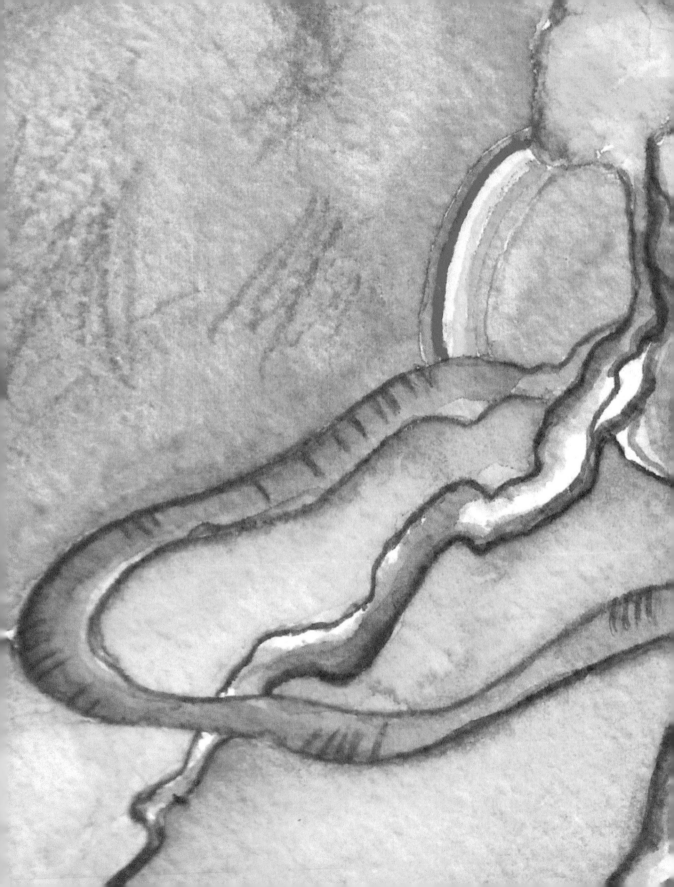

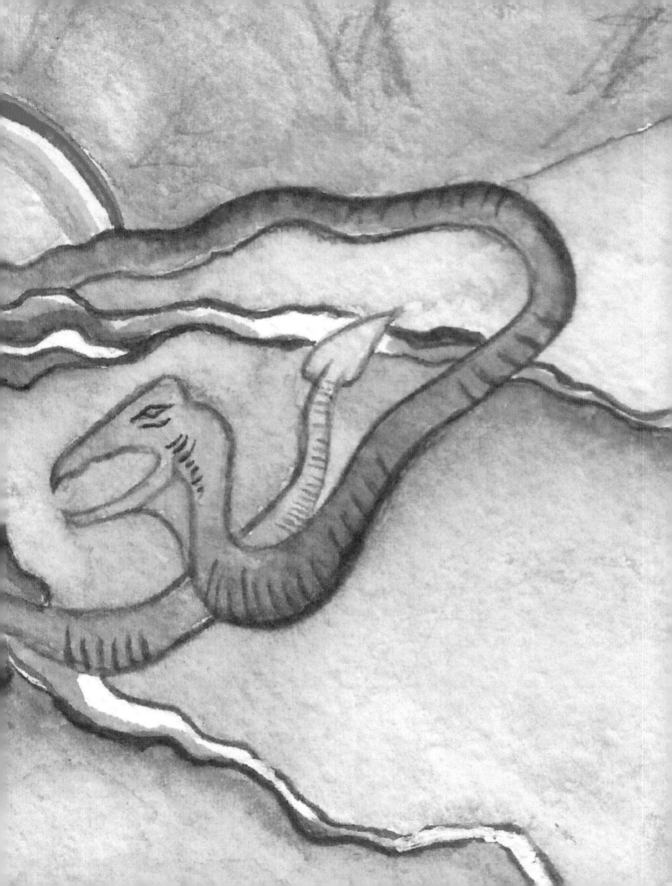

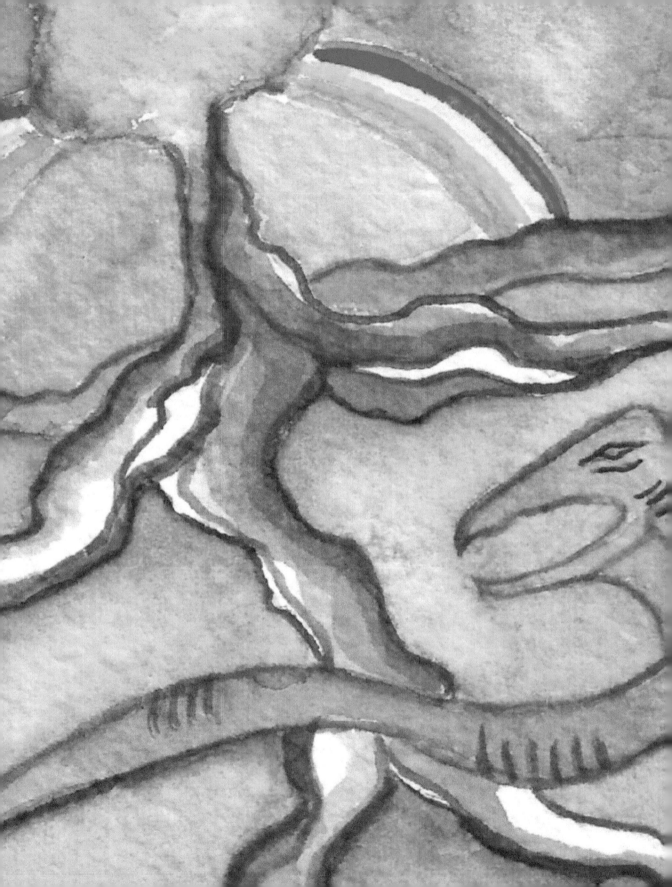

in the north, and it's sometimes confused with the world of the dead.

The tree is the most important entity in the Universe. If it dies, everything dies, including the realm of the gods. The tree needs cure and protection, because it is attached from above and below. In fact, the tree offers shelter to many beings who protect it, draw life from it, or threaten it. On its top a huge eagle perches that constantly monitors the horizon to warn the gods when their enemies are coming. Many believe that winds form whenever this eagle flaps its wings.

Four deer feed from the tree's shoots and a snake nestles at its roots constantly fighting the eagle. The squirrel, Ratatoskr, runs up and down the tree's barks to report the insults the eagle and the snake exchange with each other.

On the top of Yggdrasil rests Víðópnir, the rooster whose crowing will announce Ragnarök, the end of the world. When this happens, Yggdrasil will tremble to let everybody know that the end of time has come.

Because of all these creatures living among its roots and branches, Yggdrasil would dry up and rot. Thanks to the Norns though, who pour water from the Urdhr spring on the trunk and branches every day, Yggdrasil can can live.

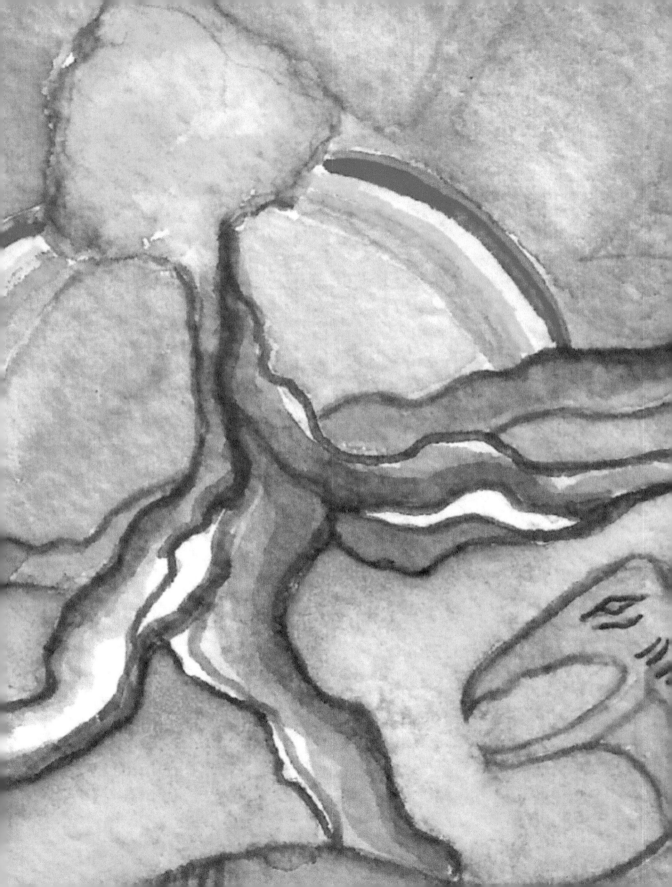

The gods like to travel up and down to the realm of humankind. They can do that by walking on a shimmering rainbow bridge called Bifröst made magically from fire, water, and air.

Thanks to the fire that burns without ceasing, Giants cannot cross over it. There is also a god, Heimdallr, standing guard over it. Also known as the White god, he can see for over a hundred miles and he can hear the growing of grass on the ground and the growing of wool on sheep.

He has gold teeth and an immense horn (the Gjallar-Horn) that he blows to announce the coming and going of the gods. Its sound can be heard in all the worlds.

The gods also use this Bridge to have their councils

in a realm called Urdar Well, situated at the foot of the Yggdrasil.

THE GOLDEN APPLES

You will probably be surprised to learn that the gods were not immortal. Their eternal youth was due to a truly precious fruit they ate: the golden apples. This fruit kept them beautiful, full of vigor and without a wrinkle. Besides, we know that an apple a day keeps the doctor away. One more reason to include apples in our daily snack.

The keeper of the magic fruit was Idun, the goddess of spring and rejuvenation. She was the wife of Bragi, the god of poetry. They were a perfect couple: while Idun fed men with the nectar of poets, Bragi fed them with the nectar of immortality.

Idun kept the golden apples in a treasure chest and give it to them every morning. One day, though, something very dangerous happened...but let's start the tales from the beginning.

One day, Odin, Loki, and Hoenir were traveling to the land of men. Tired of walking and hungry, they stopped to arrange a cookout. They killed an ox and began to cook it, but the meat always remained raw, while their belly began to grumble.

An eagle, who watched them from the top of a tree with a watchful eye, offered them a deal: if he received his portion of meat, he would release them from the spell. The three gods were already a little annoyed, but having no alternative, they agreed. The eagle, without being told twice, swooped down and took the best part of the ox and began to devour it under the angry gaze of the gods.

Loki, who was already blind from hunger, became angrier than the others and broke off a branch which he threw against the eagle. The branch remained in the body of the eagle but it rose in flight dragging with it the poor dangling Loki, giving him a hard time.

The damned eagle was flying dangerously low and Loki almost broke in two as he was begging him to let him go. It was only then that the raptor blackmailed him. He would only let him go if he gave him Idun and her precious golden apples. The second identity

of the mysterious eagle was now clear: it could only be a giant in disguise.

Willing or not, the pact was sanctioned, and on their return, Loki went to see the goddess to tell her that he had seen a fruit with powers far superior to the golden apples.

He recommended her to follow him outside the walls of Asgard with his basket of apples to see which fruit was more powerful.

Idun trusted him with hope, but as soon as he was outside, the eagle flew towards her and kidnapped her, taking her to the giant's dwelling on the top of the frozen mountains.

Without the magic apples, the gods suddenly began to age, their hair turned

gray, their skin dull and wrinkled, their eyes puffy and tired, their backs more and more hunched. A complete disaster!

Gathered in council, they began to investigate the disappearance of the beautiful Idun and immediately came to the conclusion that the last person to have seen her was Loki.

Anxious to regain their immortality, they tortured him with questions, and in the end, the cunning god revealed the misdeed. The gods were mad, but the damage was done. The only possible solution was to force Loki to bring the goddess safely home. The

alternative would have been death for him.

Freyja, the goddess of love, lent him her hawk feathers, and he, disguised as a hawk, flew off to Jotunheim, the homeland of the giants. When he arrived at his destination he found Idun alone, so he could free her easily. He turned her into a nut, and small as she had become, he had no difficulty grabbing her with his claws and bringing her home safe and sound.

As he soared with the goddess and her precious apples, the giant returned home and noticed the disappearance. Furious, he quickly transformed into an eagle, and set off in pursuit.

The hawk flew quickly, but for the eagle, the queen of the skies, it was not difficult to catch up. Loki could almost feel his breath on his neck, but all the gods watching were cheering for him. They also realized he needed help, so they lit a fire around Asgard. Loki and the beautiful Idun were just in time to pass by and feel the heat of the flames, and immediately the fire spread. The eagle (or rather the giant...) fell into it and burnt to death.

Idun and his apples were safe! The gods were in seventh heaven. Their eternal youth was preserved, they could sleep soundly again and look at themselves in the mirror with a smile.

AESIR AND VANIR

The gods of the Norse look like ordinary people. They have the same faults that people have, like jealously and temper. They also have fights and wars.

They belong to two main clans: the Aesir and the Vanir. Odin, Frigg, Thor, Loki, Balder, Hod, Heimdall and Tyr are the most influential members of the Aesir clan and are recognized as the core gods. The second tribe, Vanir, includes the gods of fertility, and counts Njord, Freyr, and Freyja as their most notable members. These two tribes usually live in peace, but once they started a bloody war that lasted a long time and ended with a truce.

ODIN,
THE KING OF GODS

- Odin is the father and king of all gods.

- He is the god of war and death, but also of the sky, wisdom and magic.

- His wife is Frigg, the goddess of fertility.

- His animal companions are two ravens, two wolves, and a horse.

- His day of the week is Wednesday.

His two ravens are named Hugin (Thought) and Munin (Mind). Every day they fly around the world spying on humans, creatures, and gods. They return to Odin each evening, and report everything they saw.

His 8-legged horse is called Sleipnir. He is his faithful companion of adventures that takes him around the world at a fast gallop in seek of adventures.

At his feet, Odin has two loyal wolves, Geri (Greedy) and Freki (Ravenous). They keep him company, guarding the border against the giants.

To be able to see the cosmos more clearly, Odin sacrificed one of his eyes. He hanged from the World Tree, Yggdrasil, for nine days and nine nights until he acquierd the knowledge of the runic alphabet.

ODIN DISCOVERING THE RUNES

Odin is a tireless seeker of knowledge and would be willing to do anything to satisfy his thirst for wisdom. It's because of these qualities that he is the god of wisdom. One of the myths that proves this is the precious discovery of the runes, the original Norse alphabet.

In the depths of the well of Ur, at the base of the Yggdrasil tree, live the Norns, three young women who can read the destiny of men and transform it, engraving the magical runes on the trunk of the Yggdrasil tree.

Odin, who observes them from the top of his divine throne, is dying to learn this magical technique guarded by the young maidens. But the knowledge of the runes is very secret, and can be transferred only to beings who truly deserve it. It's a knowledge so precious that even the god of wisdom, the king of gods, must prove himself worthy of it.

To show them his tremendous wish and abilities, Odin decided to prove himself. He hung himself from a branch of Yggdrasil, for nine days and nights, without eating and drinking any water, piercing himself with his spear, and peered downward into the shadowy waters below. He was calling to the runes for nine days and nights. The last night, they listened to him and accepted to show themselves and their deep mystery.

With the knowledge of the magical mystery of the runes Odin increased his power, he learned the unknowable and other magical secrets of the universe including how to transform destiny.

ODIN'S EYE

Odin is a very wise god, his desire for knowledge is infinite and he is willing to make great sacrifices in order to expand his horizons. Another proof is the following myth, which tells us how Odin sacrificed his eye to acquire the knowledge of truth.

Once a wise creature lived in the world, Mimir, who was even wiser than him. But how could Mimir have this immense knowledge? Well, he had a secret. Every day he drank at a well that was located at the roots of the Yggdrasill tree. The water from this well was magical and opened his mind. Odin, who as we know, was very curious, so he went to visit him and asked if he could get a sip of that magical water. But Mimir, who knew the value of that spring, asked him something really precious in exchange: he asked him to give up an eye!

Odin did not hesitate. He plucked out one eye and threw it into the depths of the well. Mimir drew a course and filled it to the brim with his magical waters. Odin drank it greedily and from then on, he became even wiser.

The myth of Odin reveals so much to us. Sometimes to understand things from a different perspective we have to close our eyes and look inside ourselves.

FRIGG, GODDESS OF MARRIAGE

- She is the celestial bride of Odin, she is the "wisest of the goddesses".

- She is the goddess of marriage and motherhood.

- She has the power of clairvoyance, but never reveals what she sees.

- She wears a large blue cape that symbolizes the sky.

- The day Friday was named after her and so Friday is considered the best day to get married on.

As the Queen of the goddesses, Frigg has a group of assistants around her. Fulla, her personal attendant, has a gold band in her hair. She looks after her special ash box and all her shoes. Gna is her second attendant and she is her messenger. Hlin is the third attendant and her role is to protect people.

Like Odin, she is entitled to sit on the royal throne, Hliðskjálf. From this throne, she and Odin can see what was happening in the nine worlds.

Frigg has his own palace, called Fensalir. To this place she invited married couples who led virtuous lives so that they could enjoy the company of their partners after death.

She is a beautiful and tall dune goddess, very fond

of jewels and luscious dresses. She changes the color of her dress based on her mood which can be very erratic.

She has the hobby of weaving clouds with a magic spinning wheel such that they glow in the dark. For this reason, the Vikings called the constellation we know as "Orion's Belt" "Frigg's Spinning Wheel".

HEL,
QUEEN OF THE DEAD

- She is the Queen of the realm of the dead.

- She is the daughter of Loki.

- She is half blue and half flesh-colored and often has a gloomy expression.

- She has a dog named Garmr.

The realm where Hel lives is also called Niflheim. It's located at the roots of the tree of life. It's a place of darkness and cold enveloped by a perpetual mist. In it dwells the dragon Níðhöggr, which gnaws endlessly at the roots of the evergreen ash tree, Yggdrasil. He also devotes himself to tormenting the souls left in the world.

She has a dog, named Garmr, who howls every time new people arrive.

THOR,
THE GOD OF THUNDER

Odin had a son who he was very proud of:

he was strong and combative. His name

was Thor, the god of thunder:

- He is the god of thunder and lightning.

- Has red hair and a full beard.

- He is quick-tempered.

- He is always hungry.

- His day of the week is Thursday.

- He is married to the goddess Sif.

- Thor travels in a chariot drawn by two goats.

- He is the strongest of the Aesir.

He wields a short-handled war hammer, the most powerful weapon in all the Nine Worlds, capable of crushing even mountains. When Thor throws it in the air, it magically returns to his hand.

He has a pair of gauntlets, a staff and a belt, which doubles his strength when he wears them. Thor is the protector of men and his enemies are a bitter serpent and the giants, as the following myths tell.

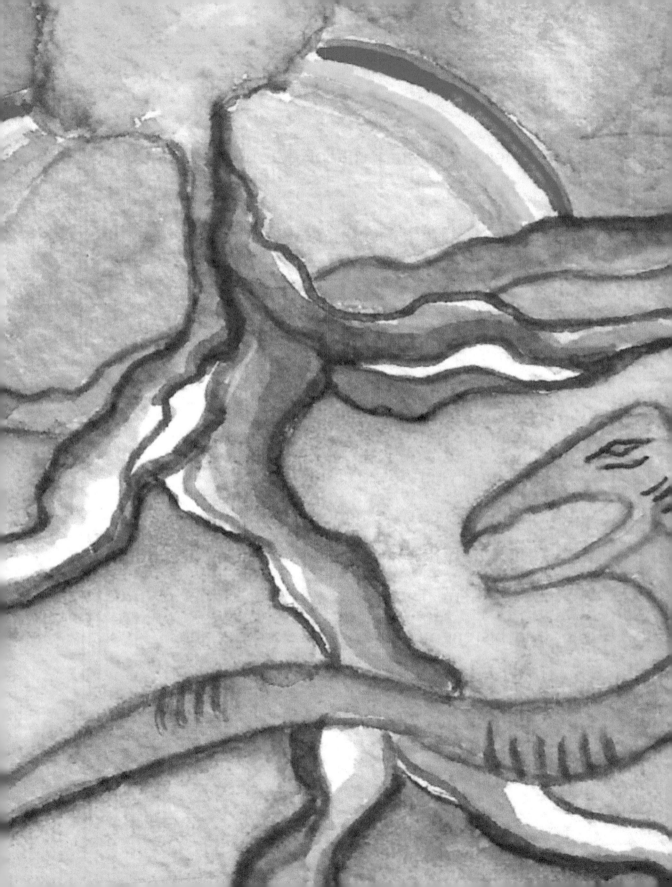

THOR AGAINST THE WORLD SERPENT

The myth tells that around the world of men, Middle Earth, there is an immense sea snake, called Jörmungandr, so long that it wraps around its entire diameter and bites its own tail.

It's the son of Loki and the giantess Angrboða, but when it was born Odin did't like it at all. He was already sure that he would bring much trouble. To get rid of him, he decided to throw him into the depths of the ocean. But the baby snake didn't want to stay there all alone in the sea. Although he was just born, he had already reached a considerable size, and it was not easy to move him. So, Odin had to call the strongest of the gods, the mythical Thor, to get help in the enterprise. And so it was that the serpent of the world was dragged by Thor in the deep abysses where it grew until it wrapped Middle Earth in its frightening embrace.

The serpent will never forget what Thor did to it, and the two will be bitter enemies forever.

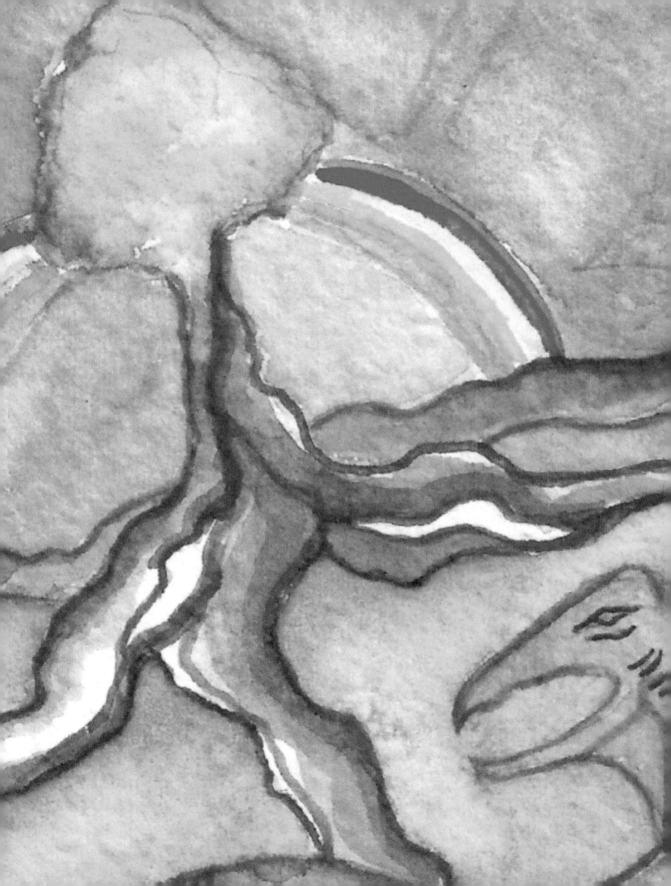

THOR'S FISHING

One day Thor was fishing with the giant
Hymir. There has always been bad blood
between the two because Thor had always
been the arch-enemy of the giants. With
Hymir though, he tried to become friends.
All of a sudden Thor felt that the hook was
pulling with too much strength. He tried to
resist but felt a strong tug that almost
dragged him into the sea. He used all his
energy and pulled the hook in the opposite

direction only to realize that the monstrous snake had taken the bait. The sky turned black, the sea swelled in a storm while the battle to death between the two rivals raged on. While Thor was preparing to strike the last blow with his powerful hammer against the snake, the giant Hymir, terrified by the furious struggle between the god and the monster, cut the line with his knife. Thor went on a rampage but it was too late. The snake quickly reentered the depths of the sea, making its traces disappear completely. The sky turned clear but Thor was agitated, because the enemy had escaped him by only a hair's breadth.

THOR'S HAMMER

You've probably heard of Thor's mighty hammer before. It's a really special weapon, because it can smash anything to pieces. What's more, when it's thrown, it comes back into the god's hands like a boomerang.

In this legendary story, you'll learn about the creation of this hammer and you'll get to know the dwarf craftsmen.

One day, Loki, a cunning and prankster god always ready to play tricks on the other gods, cut the blond hair of the Goddess Sif, Thor's wife, while she was sleeping. When she woke up, she was in shock and her husband went on a rampage.

He rushed on Loki and wanted to choke him with his own hands, while threatening to break all his bones. To escape his terrible death, Loki in the grip of anguish was thinking hard about how to get out of this predicament.

Fortunately, it occurred to him that he could ask the dwarf artisans for help. The dwarfs were extraordinary blacksmiths and goldsmiths, able to build precious artifacts with magical powers.

He was sure that his stunt would work, so he promised Thor that he would return with beautiful hair, much more beautiful than the original, and made of pure gold. So, he rushed to Nidavellir, the dwarf world, and asked two dwarves, the sons of the famous Ivaldi, to make it for him.

But Loki being Loki, he tricked the dwarves too: he told them that they were competing with all the artisan dwarves in a competition ordered by the gods. To participate, they had to make not one but three works. The dwarfs trusted him and created not only wonderful golden hair for Sif, but also a boat that always had a favorable wind and could be folded into a pocket.

But Loki still wasn't satisfied. He went to two other dwarves, called Brokkr and Sindre, and convinced them as well to participate in the fake contest. To appeal to their pride, he also told them that they would not be able to create such amazing works as the sons of Ivaldi. He even bet on his own head! In short, he found himself in trouble up to his neck.

In order not to lose the head that he had hastily played with, he transformed himself into a biting fly and began to disturb their work by biting them, but to no avail.

The undaunted dwarfs produced extraordinary works, such as a boar with golden bristles or a wonderful golden ring able to create duplicates of itself every ninth night. The biting fly continued to prick the industrious dwarfs, nonetheless, and in the end, it succeeded in his evil plan. By trying to keep the fly away from his eyes, Brokkr had to release his hands from the bellows. It was then when the mighty hammer was created.

The famous hammer that later became Thor's. It was capable of crushing mountains but had one imperfection: the shaft was a little too short. Despite its small imperfection, the dwarfs were satisfied with their work.

Loki returned to Asgard with the magical artifacts and showed them to the Gods. The golden hair went to Thor as a gift for his wife, Sif. The golden boar and the boat were a gift for Freyr. Odin got the magical spear and the golden ring, Thor got the powerful hammer, Mjölnir. Although the handle was short, Thor grabbed it and hefted it high. He let out a roar as thunder cracked across the sky.

The hammer immediately showed itself to be a precious instrument. The gods, now aware of Loki's phantom competition, supported the game and declared the hammer winner of the competition.
At this point, the winners, Sindri and Brokkr,

wanted Loki's head. Loki, who always found excellent excuses and could get away with anything, replied that they certainly had a right to his head, but they had no right to his neck. And since they could not detach the head without harming the neck, the head would have to remain in its place.

The dwarfs were not happy with the reasoning and began to protest. Odin was forced to make a compromise: Loki's head would remain intact but the dwarfs would sew up his mouth as a punishment.

THE GIANTS

The Giants, called Jotuns, were the chief enemies of the gods, because their lifestyle was very chaotic and undisciplined, and the gods wanted the opposite: bring order and create beauty in the world.

Many of the Aesir clan had either parent a giant or giantess. In any case, not all the

giants are big and ugly. They could be also beautiful, and normal sized. Some of the giants even had a very good relationship with the gods.

Like the gods, the giants had their own kingdom. They lived in Jotunheim, one of the nine worlds, east of Middle Earth, separated by rivers and a forest. Their place was full of forests, so no light could enter. This made their land cold and infertile. So, they mostly ate the fish in the water, and the animals from the dense forests.

The leader of the giants was Ymir. His story is terrific because he was not only the

first giant, but the first creature of the world, along with a cow named Audhumla. Since there were no other animals or plants to eat, he could only drink Audhumla's milk. But before we can tell this story, we need to talk about the origin of the Cosmos.

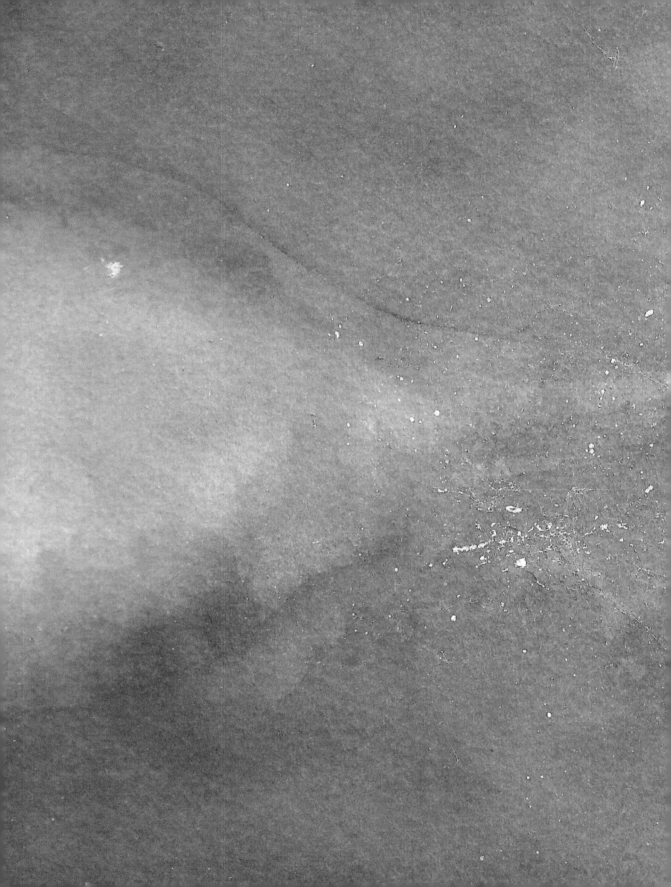

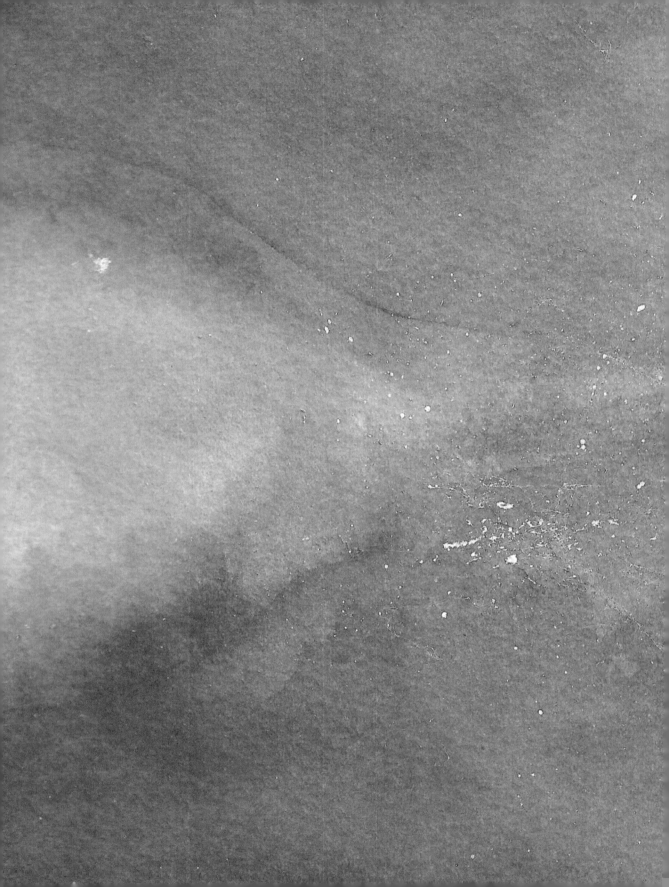

THE ORIGIN OF THE COSMOS

Ancient peoples always wondered about the origin of the cosmos. Where did the world come from? How was man born? How were the gods born? Their explanation has always been fascinating and articulate. So, get ready to start a fantastic journey full of surprises in time and space.

Norse tribes believed that before the known world, there was a bottomless abyss, called Ginnungagap. At the edge of this abyss existed a land of fire and a land of ice. Little by little, ice and fire approached each other and guess what happened.

The same thing that happens when you bring an icicle close to a flame. It first starts to melt then evaporate. The vapor turned into water, just as clouds in the sky turn into rain. This water gave rise to the first creatures: the giant Ymir, who lived

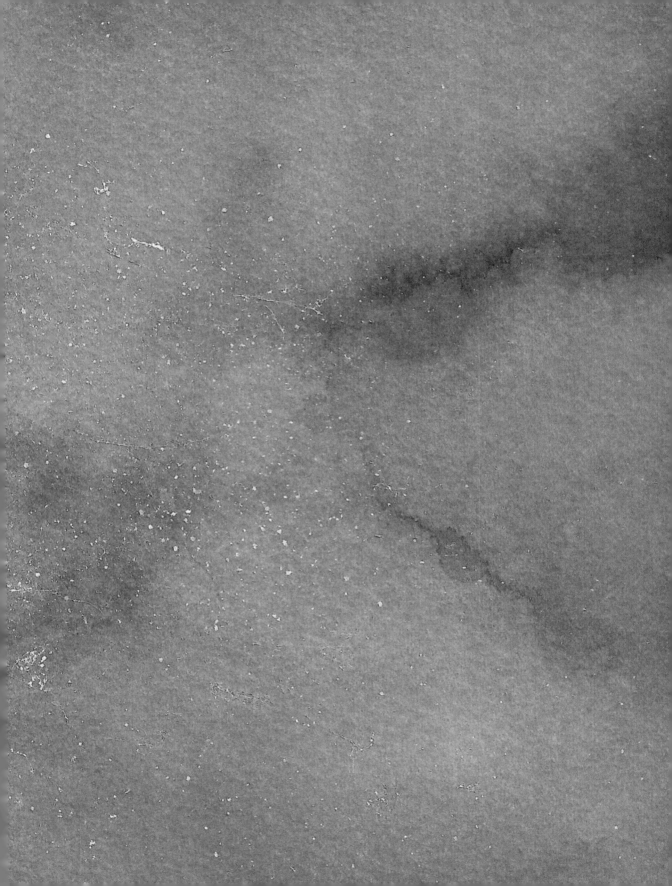

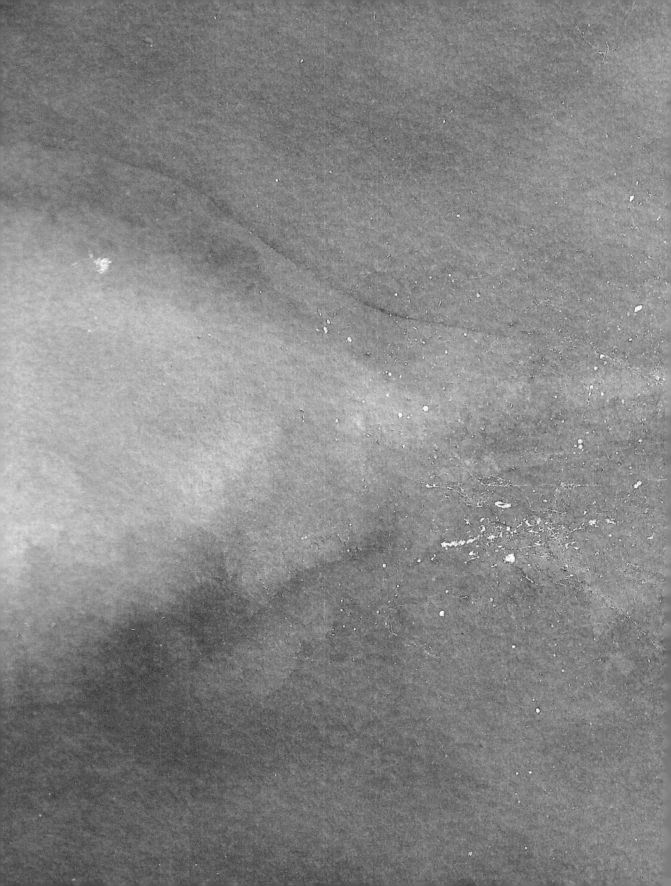

alone in these desolate lands with a cow, Audumla. Ymir has no other source of nutrition but Audumla's milk.

Ymir, being a giant, was already endowed with superpowers, and one of these was giving birth to children. A couple of children were born from under his armpits and another handful from under his legs. With all the children around, he felt less lonely, and he formed a happy family.

Ymir and his family drank Audumla's milk, but what did the poor cow have to feed on? The land where they lived was still desolate and there was nothing to eat. Audumla had no other choice but to lick the salty frost from the stones to feed herself.

One day, she found herself licking the same stone for several days. At a certain point something began to sprout from the stone: it was a hair. She didn't pay too much attention and continued to lick, only to see an entire head revealed the next day. By the third day, a body of a complete man appeared. It was Buri, the grandfather of all the gods, including Odin and his brothers.

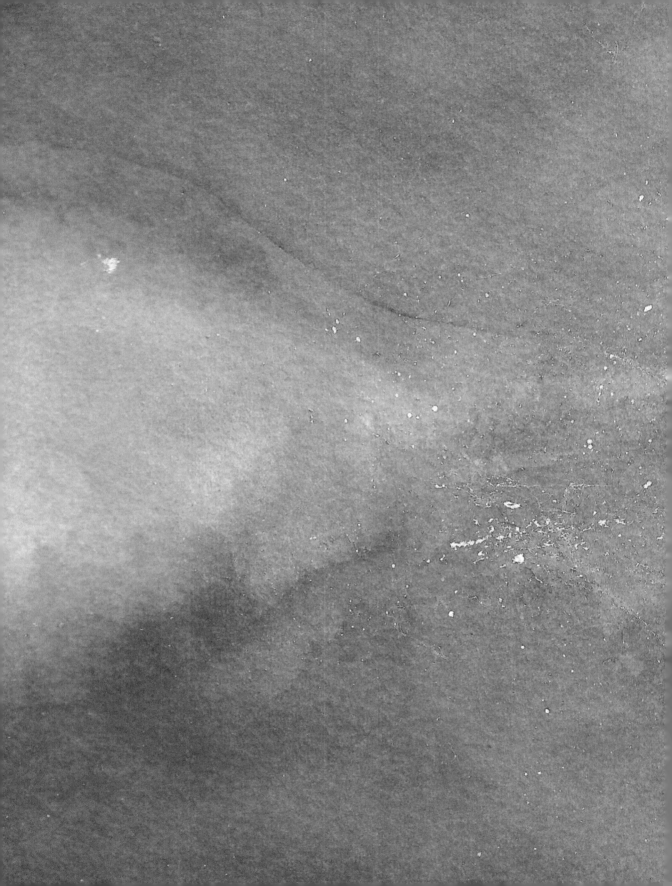

But the gods didn't like giants very much, so one day Odin and his brothers decided to kill Ymir. His body was so big that so much blood came out that it drowned all the giants. Only two were saved, Bergelmir together with his wife. From them descended the lineage of the Giants of Ice.

Odin and the gods had come to put some order in this chaotic world where almost nothing existed yet. Since Odin had special magical powers, he used Ymir's enormous body to transform it into something else.

His flesh became the earth, his blood formed lakes and rivers. Mountains were erected with his bones, his teeth became stones, and trees grew from his hair. Odin also used his body to create the vault of heaven, the stars, the wind and the clouds. His eyebrows served as material for a place where men could be safe from the giants: Middle Earth.

LOKI, GOD OF FIRE

- God of fire.

- Inveterate swindler.

- Son of a giant.

- He carried no weapons, had no special attributes other than being a shapeshifter.

He could turn into a salmon, a flea, a fly, a mare or even a human being.

Loki is present in many myths, and he is

also the protagonist of the following myth that paints him in a dark light. He was the main cause of the death of Baldur, the god of light.

THE DEATH OF BALDUR

Baldur was a very good god, and everybody loved him: he was handsome, good and generous. Because of his character, a brilliant light emanated from his body. But the god of light was not loved by all. Loki, the god of fire, was very jealous of him and wanted him dead.

One night, Baldur woke up in anguish. He had a horrible nightmare that foretold his death. He told his mother, Frigg, who asked for advice from his father, Odin.

Odin wanted to see clearly, but the only

prophetess that could help him was already dead. So, the king of all the gods, mounted his fast eight-legged steed and rushed to the underworld to consult his oracle. When he entered the icy realm of Hel, he found it festively decorated, as if they were waiting for an important guest. He summoned the prophetess who, awakened from her sleep of death, asked Odin: "Did you wake me up to find out who the infernal feast is for? It's for your beloved son, Baldur," said the prophetess. "It's his brother who will kill him. And you, Odin, will give birth to a son to avenge his death. Now let me sleep again."

Frigg, upon learning about his son's tragic future, was determined to do everything possible so that the prophecy would not come true. So, she turned to all living beings and made them promise not to harm her son; she spoke to water, fire, iron, stones, poisons and snakes.

All beings made a solemn promise not to do any harm to their beloved Baldur. To test his invulnerability, the gods formed a circle around the god and tried to throw stones, spears and all sorts of objects at him, but Baldur remained intact. The Gods were happy, except one: Loki. He got really annoyed as he was watching the gods play with him, challenging his invulnerability.

He visited Frigg, in the guise of an innocent

"Really? But everyone, literally everyone has promised?" asked the wily Loki. "Well, I didn't speak to Mistletoe, he seemed too young and harmless" replied the naive mother. This was just the information Loki needed!

He ran to get a sprig of mistletoe, and mounted it on a spear: the deadly weapon was ready. Now the archer was needed: he looked around and realized that there was a god who remained outside the circle; it was Hodr, brother of Baldur, the blind god of winter. "Why don't you play with the other gods too?" he asked him. "Because

I'm blind, I wouldn't see the target, and I don't have a weapon," replied the god. "Don't worry, I have a weapon that suits you, and I can help you aim to shoot the arrow" Loki answered.

So Hodr took a fatal hit at the god of light, pierced by the mistletoe. A cry rose to the sky, and all the gods remained silent in shock. Everyone knew who the culprit was, but now was not the time to make a scene. Frigg and Odin couldn't bear the loss. Frigg wept and implored the gods to descend into the underworld to find his beloved son and bring him back to life. Herm the Bold, Odin's son, volunteered. He mounted his father's swift steed and descended into the underworld.

While the gods mourned the death of Baldur and organized his funeral, Herm rode for nine nights until he reached the bridge that separates the realm of the living from the realm of the dead. There he encountered the guardian of the bridge, the giantess Modgud, who gave him valuable information about his brother. When the intrepid Herm arrived at the entrance of Hel, the gate was closed, but his steed took a leap that allowed him to enter. Inside he saw his brother whose heart was bursting with emotion. He would have liked to hold him tight and confess how much he had missed him, but he preferred to remain respectful of the laws of the underworld. He approached Hel and with all respect asked her to grant him the grace to bring Baldur back to life, because all creatures loved him and mourned him.

Hel, from the top of his throne, with a solemn voice

said to him: "If what you say is true, Baldur will be freed. But only if all the creatures of the universe, alive or dead, will mourn his death. If there is only one creature that doesn't mourn, Baldur will have to stay". The gods sent messengers throughout the world to see if everybody's was mourning Baldu's death. And indeed, they all were: the earth, the trees, the woodland creatures, the metals, everything. Only a giantess named Thokk refused: it was clearly the jealous Loki in disguise. All was lost, Baldur would never return.

The angry gods wanted to take revenge on Loki who was the cause of his death and sabotaged the last attempt to resurrect him. Loki ran away and hid in the woods in a house with four doors in case a quick escape is required. He even hid in the sea in a fish net, turning himself into a salmon. Eventually though, the gods managed to catch him and imprisoned him in a cave.

They turned his son Vali into a wolf. Vali mauled his brother Nari and the gods used his entrails to bind Loki to three rocks while a snake dripped acidic poison on his face. Luckily, his wife Sigyn sat next to him with a basin to collect the drops of poison and prevent them from falling on his face. But the bowl inevitably filled up, and every time she went to empty it, the drops of poison slipped on Loki's face and he shook so hard that the whole earth shook (this is what we know as an earthquake).

LOKI'S DAMNED LINEAGE

Loki was an ambiguous God, brilliant and cunning. He was a friend of the clan Aesir and he was their companion in their adventures, but at the same time he often deceived them. He fought against the gods in the final battle of Ragnarök. Loki was also responsible for producing three monstrous and terrible children: the wolf Fenrir, the serpent Jormungandr, and the goddess of death, Hel. How did this happen?

One day Loki was walking in the realm of the giants and encountered a half-roasted heart among the ashes. Since the excursion had made him very hungry, without thinking too much about it, he devoured it. Unfortunately, it was not a heart like any other, it belonged to the giantess Angrboða, whose name means "bearer of pain". Angrboða was a very strong warrior, she was the head of a tribe of wolves capable of turning into a wolf.

For some magical reason, a few months later Loki realized, to his amazement, that he was pregnant. When the time came, he gave birth to three children: the first was a wolf (Fenrir), the second one was a snake (Jormungand), and the third one was a girl with a face divided in half: one part looked normal, the other part was the color of death: purple and withered. He named her Hel.

When the Aesir learned about these three

monstrous children, they didn't trust Loki because of all the trouble he had caused in the past. They were certain that only misfortune and pain would come from them. This made Odin want to get rid of them, so he ordered the Aesir to go to the world of the giants where the evil offspring were raised, and bring them to him. First, he tried to get rid of the serpent and throw it into the outer ocean that surrounds all lands. But it was not an easy task. He had to ask for help from his son, Thor, because the snake had an extraordinary strength.

In the end, they managed to get rid of him, but in the depths of the abyss the serpent continued to grow until it surrounded the whole world and bit its own tail. We already know from our previous tale that this serpent was one of the most bitter enemies of Thor who tried to kill it several times.

Then Odin took care of Hel. Instead of killing her, he assigned her a task: she became the lady of all the dead that died of illness or old age.

As for the wolf Fenrir, his life was also spared even though the gods knew he would try to kill Odin. They tried to change his destiny by raising him in Asgard. As we will see later, Tyr managed to develop a relationship with him that kept him bound.

FREYR, GOD OF FERTILITY

- Freyr is the god of peace, fertility and abundance.

- Son of the sea god Njörd and brother of the goddess Freya.

- He rules the realm of Alfheimr where the elves live.

- Freyr rules over rain, sun and harvest.

He rides a golden boar and owns a ship that always has the wind in its favor and can be folded and carried in a pocket. Both are gifts from the dwarf artisans, commissioned by Loki to make up for stealing Sif's golden hair (see chapter 'Thor's Hammer'). One of the most beautiful myths featuring Freyr is the myth of his love for Gerd.

GERD'S COURTSHIP

One day Freyr sat on the throne of Hlidskjalf, the high throne of Odin and Friss, from which he could see everything that happened in the nine worlds.

He looked towards the north, the land of the Jotunheim giants, and his gaze rested on an exceptionally beautiful girl, a giantess called Gerd. He saw her walking towards a dwelling, and when she lifted

hers arms to open the door, a light illuminated the sky, the sea, and the whole universe.

Freyr fell madly in love with her in a single moment. When he got home, he could not help thinking about her: he didn't speak, he didn't sleep, he didn't want to drink anything and no one dared to speak to him. This was the price he paid for sitting on the sacred throne, on which only Odin and his queen could sit.

Determined to marry her, he sent her his faithful servant, Skirnir. He asked for Frey's precious sword in return, a sword so special that it could fight by itself. But that wasn't enough, Skrinir also wanted Freyr's magical steed capable of crossing flames.

Skirnir rode all night to see Gerd, but her place was guarded by wild dogs. Skirnir asked a shepherd how he could enter, but the shepherd tried to talk him out of going any further. Luckily, the giantess heard some noises, noticed Skirnir and invited him in. Skirnir introduced himself and was warmly welcomed, but he had a hard time convincing Gerd to marry Freyr. First, Skirnir tried to persuade her with the most generous gifts including the eleven golden apples of immortality, and the powerful ring of Odin, but the girl resisted. He even tried to convince her by force, threatening her with the sword of Freyr, but to no avail.

Gerd surrendered only in front of the magic of the runes, which foretold the wrath of the gods and horrible misfortunes if she did not marry the god. The union between the two took place after nine nights in secret.

FREYJA, GODDESS OF LOVE

- She is the goddess of love, beauty and seduction.

- She is the twin sister of Freyr and the wife of Odr.

- She is a seer and an expert in the magical arts.

- She has two beautiful daughters, Gorsimi and Hnoss, whose names mean "treasure".

Odr often leaves for long journeys leaving her alone, and she in the throes of love, cries tears of red gold for him and seeks him relentlessly.

She rides a chariot pulled by two cats, and is accompanied by the boar Hildisvíni who protects her in wars. She has a cloak made of hawk feathers which allows her to turn into any bird and to fly in the sky at will. She wears the Brísingamen necklace made by the dwarves. It represents the sun and the passage from day to night.

Freyja reigns over Fólkvangr, a field where half of those who die in battle go, while the other half go to Valhalla ruled by Odin.

THE VALKYRIES

The Valkyries are a group of maidens in Odin' service. Their task is to decide which soldiers die in battle. They ride white winged horses and are armed with helmets and spears.

Odin and Freyia decide which soldiers should die with honor and so the Valkyries take them to Valhalla, ruled by Odin or Fólkvangr, ruled by Freyja. There the fallen

soldiers fight each other every day to prepare to help Odin and Freyja in the final battle of Ragnarök. Their wounds which they receive during these fights heal in the evening when they celebrate. They drink mead, the drink of the gods made of from honey and served by the Valkyries.

NJORD, THE GOD OF SEA

- Njord is the god of wind and seas.

- He is the protector of sailors and fishermen.

- He calms storms, helps ships in distress and blows favorable winds.

- He lives above the sea in a realm known as Nóatún.

- He is a Vanir deity and father of Freyr and Freya.

- He joined the Aesir to seal the peace agreement.

THE UNHAPPY MARRIAGE BETWEEN NJORD AND SKADI

One day the sea god married the giantess Skadi, but their marriage was not happy for many different reasons. Here's what happened:

Let's recall what happened when a giant kidnapped the beautiful Idun (see chapter 'The Golden Apples'), and in the guise of an eagle inflicted harm on her. Odin, Loki and Thor took revenge by killing the giant who was Skadi's father. Feeling devastated and furious, Skadi wanted to avenge his father at all costs.

To calm her murderous fury, the gods offered her various reparations. First, Odin cast her father's eyes into the night sky where they turned into two stars. Second, the gods tried to break the tension by making Skadi laugh. After several vain attempts, Loki tied one end of a rope to a goat and the other end around his testicles and began a game of tug-of-war with the goat. The Giantess couldn't help but laugh.

The third reward was to give her a husband from among the Aesir. The giantess could choose one of the Gods on condition that he was covered and only his feet were visible. The gods gathered covered by a curtain showing only their feet. Skadi selected the feet that seemed to her the most beautiful of all, thinking that they were Baldur's, the most beautiful of the gods. In reality though, she had chosen Njord.

They had some differences about where to live because Njord would never leave the sea, while Skadi preferred the icy mountains of Thrymheim. In order to reach an agreement, they decided to do a trial run. They would live 9 days at the sea and 9 days in the mountains, but at the end of this trial period neither of them was happy. Skadi couldn't sleep on the seabed, because of the whining of the waterfowl, and Njord didn't like the mountains where Skadi lived, as they were dark and threatening. What's more, he couldn't stand the howling of the wolves. Eventually they had to give up and decided by mutual agreement to live apart.

TYR, AND THE CHAIN OF FENRIR

- Tyr is the ancient god of war and the lawgiver of the gods.

- He is the bravest of the gods: the god of justice.

- His day is Tuesday.

- He is endowed with superhuman

strength, but he is also extremely intelligent, wise, and cunning.

- He is a born diplomat and for this reason he is considered more than the god of war.

Tyr is known for a story that perfectly represents his personality as the god of justice.

One day the gods decided to raise a wolf cub called Fenrir, Loki's son. The gods already knew his destiny and knew that he would become a ferocious wolf, but they tried to change him. None of them, however, had the courage to approach him to feed him, except Tyr. So, with his help, the wolf grew and started to become more and more dangerous until the gods felt it was time to tie him up. But it wasn't such an easy task, as Fenrir broke all the chains. The gods then decided to turn to the dwarves who we already know to be excellent blacksmiths.

The dwarves forged the magical Gleipnir, an indestructible chain made of six mystical materials: the sound of a cat's paw, a woman's beard, the roots of a mountain, the sinews of a bear, the breath of a fish, and the saliva of a bird. The chain also seemed as thin and soft as silk.

When the Gods tried to chain Fenrir with this thin, soft material, the wolf became suspicious: there is no way the gods think this fragile chain can keep him tied up unless there is some trickery involved.

In the end, he accepted but on the condition that one of the gods puts his hand in his mouth while tied up. If they were lying, one of the gods would lose a hand. Týr volunteered. The chain became very strong when Fenrir tried to free himself. Realizing that he had been tricked, Fenrir bit off Týr's hand in anger.

THE WAR BETWEEN THE AESIR AND THE VANIR

As we already mentioned, the gods of the Norse mythology did not belong to one tribe but to two different families, the Aesir and the Vanir. They lived in two different kingdoms. The Aesir lived in Asgard and the Vanir lived in Vanaheim.

The two different families had always lived happily until a conflict broke out between them. This can be considered the first war in the world. But let's take a step back to find out what happened.

At that time Freyja, the goddess of love and beauty, belonged to the tribe of Vanir and she was passionate about the art of magic. To practice her magic, she would wonder all the realms in disguise.

One day, curious to find out what the Aesir were thinking, she crossed the rainbow bridge and introduced herself to them with the name of Heith, meaning 'bright'. The gods welcomed her kindly and noticed that she could shape one's destiny with magic, so the gods began to ask her all sorts of favors.

Unfortunately, the gods were not so different from humans. If we had the power to grant all our wishes, what would we ask for? How would our future look? Would it look better? We would probably get greedy and we couldn't stop asking for things. The Aesir gods did the same: they went too far with their requests, and when they realized, it was too late.

The solution was simple: find a culprit! They agreed it was Freyja's fault, she was a witch, and she had to be burned. And so it happened that they started to call her Gullveig ("Gold-drunk") and set fire under her feet. This is what Freyja got for doing nothing but fulfilling the gods' desires.

Luckily Freyja was more powerful than they thought. Every time she was burned, she was reborn from her own ashes. They tried three times, but in the end, they had to give up, Freyja was reborn again.

This incident created hostility between the two

families and marked the beginning of a war that was fought for a long time. The Aesir used only weapons to fight their opponents in battle, while the Vanir also used magic. Eventually, the two tribes came to an agreement and exchanged some hostages. Freyja, Freyr and Njord (of the Vanir tribe) went to the Aesir, while Hoenir and Mimir went to the Vanir.

After some time, the Vanir realized that Hoenir (the god of silence, spirituality, poetry and passion) wasn't a very good decision maker, he would always ask Mimir for any advice. They began to think that they had overestimated him and became very angry.

The gods of Vanir thought the hostages had not been properly exchanged: the Aesir received three gods with extraordinary powers, while they got two gods, one of which was somewhat inferfior to the others. To take revenge, they cut off Mimir's head and sent it back to the Aesir.

Odin was shocked, as he cared deeply for Mimir. Let's recall the time he went to drink from t fountain of wisdom in exchange for his eye. To preserve it, he embalmed it with herbs and sang magical poems to him. Odin managed to keep Mimir's head alive who continued to give indispensable advice to Odin in times of need.

SOL AND MANI

Among the Nordic peoples, the sun and the moon were two deities, brother and sister. The sun, Sol, was the sister of the moon, Mani. The two of them, along with all the stars, were originated by sparks from the land of fire (Muspelheim), and ascended to the heavens in riderless chariots.

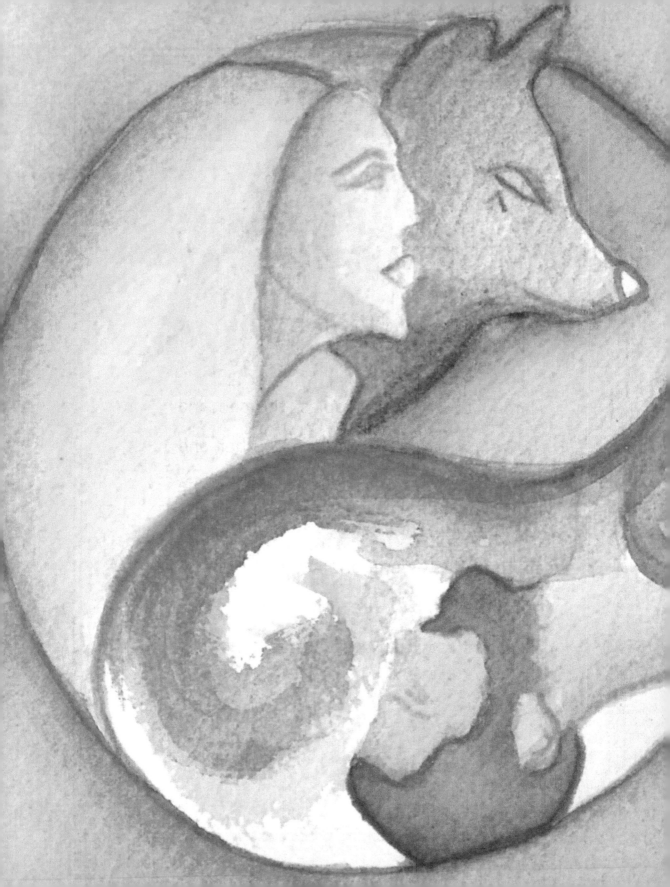

At the beginning, they were a bit confused not knowing very well how to move and what their mission in life was. Then the gods formed a council to organize the different parts of day and night, the year and the cycles of the moon. Both the sun and the moon rode in the sky on horse-drawn chariots; they moved fast because they were chased by two wolves who wanted to devour them. But they will only succeed when the chaos of Ragnarök comes: the end of time total darkness.

BIL AND HJÚKI, THE HELPERS OF THE MOON

One evening, Mani the moon got tired of always working alone to regulate the phases of the moon, so he looked towards the Earth in search of help. His gaze fell on two brothers, Bil and Hjúki. The two children had gone to collect water from a well and they were returning home carrying a bucket and a stick. They could help out, thought Mani, so he kidnapped them and took them with him in the sky. Even now, if we look carefully, we can make out the two brothers on the lunar disk with their bucket called Søgr and their stick called Símul.

THE MYSTERIOUS ELVES

The elves were mysterious creatures ruled by Freyr, the god of the sun and summer. They were divided into two different races: the Liósálfar, the light elves, and the Døkkálfar, the dark elves.

The light elves were beautiful and good and lived in the fairy realm of Alfhein which means the land of the elves. With their knowledge of magic they could help

people, but they could cause harm and diseases, too.

Light elves also provided inspiration to people for artistic creation, and were considered guardian angels. The elves managed the five elements and they could go through them. They loved nature which they protected, and felt at one with.

Dark elves were generally evil in nature. They were dark and ugly, so they were condemned to hide and live underground in the realm of Svartálfaheimr so that nobody could see them. If they were to come out in daylight, they were turned into stone. Dark elves annoyed and threatened humans. One of their favorite activities was to sit on the chest of sleeping people to evoke bad dreams.

THE INDUSTRIOUS DWARVES

Along with the dark elves lived the dwarves in Svartálfaheimr. They had many characteristics in common with the dark elves, like being short and ugly, and if they came out into the sunlight they also turned to stone.

They had a colossal strength, so the four corners of the sky were held by four dwarfs: Austri, Vestri, Nordri and Sudri ("East", "West", "North" and "South").

The dwarves were skilled craftsmen, capable of creating artifacts that were not only incredibly beautiful but also endowed with magical powers, such as Mjollnir, Thor's hammer. It was capable of smashing mountains and it always came back after striking a blow.

Then there was Skidbladnir, Freyr's ship, that always had a favorable wind and could be folded and stored in a breast pocket. It was the dwarves who created Odin's unbeatable spear that never missed a blow, and they made his Draupnir ring, a magical ring capable of multiplying itself. They also created Brisingamen, Freyja's magnificent necklace; and Sif's, Thor's wife's long golden hair.

THE NORNS, LADIES OF FATE

The Norns are female spirits who shape the destiny of the gods and men. They engrave the runes with the letters of the ancient Norse alphabet. If somebody learns this alphabet, they can change their destiny. That's why Odin did everything to gain this knowledge hanging for days on

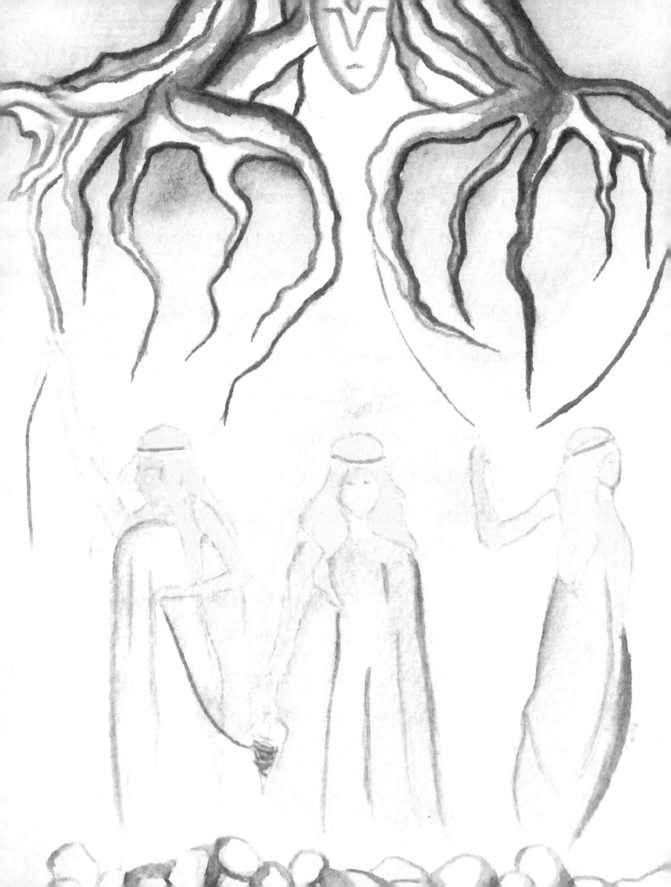

the tree of the world.

There are three main Norns: Urðr, meaning "what was", Verðandi "what is becoming" and Skuld "what will be". They represent the past, the present and the future.

In addition to these three major Norns, there are numerous minor Norns with various powers over the fate of people. Some of them, for example, visit newborns and assign each of them a fate. These creatures can be good or evil which explains why the fate of people are so different from each other.

The Norse reside at Urd, the well of destiny at the roots of the world tree. They have the very important task of watering Yggdrasil with water drawn from that well and clay to prevent it from drying out or rotting.

The weave a loom which is composed of many threads. Each individual's life corresponds to one of these threads, and its length determines the length of his or her life. They don't only govern the lives of humans, but also of plants, and of every creature.

Even the Gods are subject to their fate and they are not immortal. In fact, many of them perish in the final battle of Ragnarök. The only creatures that we can consider immortal are the Norns.

The Norns have an equivalent in both Greek and Roman mythology. They were known as Moire by the Greeks and Fates by the Romans.

RAGNARÖK, THE FATE OF THE GODS

Ragnarök was a catastrophic event that caused the destruction of the entire known world, including the gods. The gods were aware, thanks to the prophecies, that this event would happen, even if they were not aware of the exact moment at which it would happen. Nonetheless, they prepared every day to face it.

Ragnarök means destiny of the gods indicating its inevitability. The final battle was fought between the Aesir gods led by Odin, the fire giants, Loki and all monstrous creatures that will be freed from their chains.

This is how it will begin. One day, decreed by the Norns, the spinners of our destiny, it will start to get colder and colder, and very cold winters will follow one another. It will be snowing constantly, biting wind will blow in all directions, and tremendous ice will cover the entire Earth.

The sun will be swallowed up by Skoll, the wolf, who has been chasing it to devour it. The moon will have the same fate, as another wolf, Hati, will swallow it. Even the stars in the sky will go out. Summer will no longer come, it will just be a succession of cold winters for three years.

The cosmic tree Yggdrasill will shake and the land

will tremble, mountains will fall to the ground, volcanoes will explode and wild beasts will run wild through the villages. Humans, not knowing what to eat, will be so desperate that they will begin to kill each other. All moral laws will fall, the brother will kill his own brother, the father his son and the son his father.

Jormungand, the Midgard Serpent will rise up from the depths of the ocean and fly to the shore, causing tidal waves and swells. He will release a poison so deadly that it will blow up the sky and the sea.

The ferocious wolf Fenrir will break free from his chains and unleash hell: flames will burst from his eyes and nostrils and he will open his jaws so wide that his upper jaw will lean against the sky and his lower one against the Earth.

Fire and flames will rage, for the sons of Muspelheim, the fire realm, led by the fire giant Surt, with his sword of fire brighter than the sun, will advance towards the other realms, destroying everything they encounter, including the marvelous Bifröst Bridge, which will collapse beneath their feet.

Heimdallr, the guardian of the rainbow bridge, will blow his horn to call for the final confrontation.

The fire giants will advance towards the Vígríðr plain where the final battle will take place. They will be joined by Fenrir, the Midgard serpent, the frost giants, and Loki, who in the meantime managed to free himself from his chains and was eager to take revenge for the wrong done to him by the gods.

Also the sailing ship Naglfar, built with the nails of the dead, will sail towards Vígríðr ferrying the forces of chaos that will be in battle with the gods.

In the final battle, in which the heroes of Valhalla will also take part, the wolf Fenrir will devour Odin, but will be avenged by his son Viðarr. Thor will manage to kill the monstrous sea serpent Jormungand, but will die shortly thereafter from his injuries.

The god of war Týr will fight Garmr, the hellhound who guarded the entrance to Hel, but they both die. The fire giant Surtr will defeat Freyr after a long and hard fight, after which he will set fire to the world with his sword. Only a couple of humans will be saved by taking refuge in a forest and will make rebirth possible, repopulating the Earth. Only a few gods will survive, such as the sons of Odin, Viðarr and Váli, and the sons of Thor, Móði and Magni, who will inherit the powers of their fathers, and the beloved Baldur will rise from hell, giving the world the hope of a new beginning.

The sun will have begotten a daughter who will shine from the heavens, and the eternal cycle of life will be born anew.

Made in the USA
Coppell, TX
04 February 2023

12204966R00096